The Last of the Dragons

by Kristin Walter

A Samuel French Acting Edition

SAMUEL FRENCH
FOUNDED 1830

SAMUELFRENCH.COM

ISBN 978-0-87440-258-2 Printed in U.S.A. #B1496

THE LAST OF THE DRAGONS was originally produced in March of 2006 by Manhattan Children's Theatre. It was directed by Laura Stevens with set design by Aaron Mastin and costume design by Cully Long. The cast was as follows:

PRINCESS . . . . Lisanne Marie
PRINCE . . . . David Demato
KING . . . . Chris Alonzo
NURSE . . . . Chelsea Palano
VALET . . . . B.J. Thorne
DRAGON . . . . Alex Rasovar

CHARACTERS

Princess
Prince
King
Nurse
Valet
Dragon

SETTING

The play takes place in both the interior and exterior of a castle, and in the dragon's lair on the outskirts of town.

Scene One
The Palace Interior

(Music. All enter and begin to dance, forming patterns and weaving in and around each other. They freeze in tableau. The music continues to underscore **STORYTELLER.***)*

STORYTELLER. Once, long ago, the skies were filled with dragons. Huge, scaly, fire-breathing beasts with wings like bats' wings, but a hundred times bigger. And they had a taste for royal blood. Whenever a princess turned sixteen, a dragon would swoop into the castle and carry her off to his lair. Oh, but never fear! While the sweet, helpless princess wailed and cowered in the corner, a brave young prince would slay the dragon and carry her off to his kingdom to be married. Ah, such a romantic tale!

Well…it's romantic for some.

Here in the kingdom of Middlefield, they are all about to learn an important lesson about dragons. For the princess is about to turn sixteen. And she is a different sort of princess.

Scene Two
The Princess's Chamber

(**PRINCESS** *is on the floor of her chamber, doing push-ups.* **NURSE** *enters.)*

NURSE. Are you ready for bed, luv?

PRINCESS. Ninety-eight...ninety nine...one hundred. Whew! I just need to brush my hair.

(**NURSE** *pulls up a chair and settles into it).*

Oh, what a day! My fencing lesson in the morning, then a hike up into the mountains. Oh, Nurse, the sky was so blue and the air so clean. I could have stayed up there forever.

NURSE. Yes, I spoke to your father this evening. He was rather put out that you didn't come to the tea party.

PRINCESS. Tea party? Oh! That was today?

NURSE. All the girls in the village were there.

PRINCESS. I wondered why the marketplace seemed so quiet. Not a single giggle.

NURSE. Now, your highness, you need to select your maid of honor soon.

PRINCESS. But I don't like any of the village girls. All they ever want to do is wear fancy dresses and gossip. I can't even find one who will arm wrestle.

NURSE. Well, you can't put it off much longer.

PRINCESS. I know.

NURSE. You're almost sixteen.

PRINCESS. I know.

NURSE. Your wedding is coming up very soon.

PRINCESS. I know.

NURSE. And that reminds me! Bedtime story!

PRINCESS. Oh, no, can't we forget about it just this once?

NURSE. It's tradition. I cannot break tradition.

PRINCESS. But you have told me the same story every night for as long as I can remember. I knew it by heart before I could walk. Please, can't you tell me a different one?

NURSE. Absolutely not!

PRINCESS. I heard a wonderful story in the market yesterday about a mermaid who fell in love with a human and she trades her voice to the Sea Witch for legs…

NURSE. I must insist, your highness, that we…

PRINCESS. Well, how about that delightful tale about the pea and the hundred mattresses? It's about a princess.

NURSE. I have a duty to your father to…

PRINCESS. Snow White?

NURSE. No.

PRINCESS. Red Riding Hood?

NURSE. Sorry.

PRINCESS. Goblet of Fire?

NURSE. Since the beginning of time, there has been a great tradition in royal families from Russia to Wales. Each night, as young princes and princesses turn in for the night, they are reminded of their duty to their country and their crown. They are told the story of the dragon and…

PRINCESS. …and how it kidnaps the princess and the prince comes to rescue her and slays the dragon and they get married and everyone lives happily ever after. I know.

NURSE. Now you just lay back in that bed. This story has been passed down for thousands of years. It's as old as the stars themselves. *(begins puppet show)*

Long, long ago
When the earth was new
And the fields were green
And the sky was blue
There lived a lovely princess
As beautiful as you
In a castle near the ocean.

The princess had a mother
A selfish, awful queen

NURSE. *(cont.)* Who claimed her daughter's face
Was the prettiest 'ere seen.
She boasted to the mermaids
The mermaids all turned green
And envy is an evil emotion.

Their anger woke a dragon
Who slept beside the sea.
He vowed he'd have this princess,
The princess tried to flee.
The king cried, "You can't have her
After all, she's royalty!"
So the dragon burned down the city.

The king and queen, they pleaded
But the monstrous beast said nay.
He'd stop the slaughter if the girl
Would marry him that day.
So they tied her to a rock
To let him carry her away.
And the village wept with pity.

But at that very moment
A prince was riding by
A muscled youth with hair of gold
Eyes bluer than the sky.
He saw the helpless maiden
Who was shivering and cry-
Ing and swore that he would assist her.

The dragon swooped in roaring
And scales and daggers clashed
The blood was flowing freely
The queen and mermaids all got splashed
Our hero slew the dragon
Through the maiden's ropes he slashed
She was gorgeous, how could he resist her?

NURSE. *(cont.)* The prince and princess married that very night and they were never unhappy again. And ever since that time, no marriage of a prince and princess can take place without the slaying of a dragon.
Now, was that so terrible?

(The **PRINCESS** *gives her a look.)*

Well, it won't be just a story for much longer, my sweet. Remember, your sixteenth birthday is next week. Your father has a prince all picked out for you. He'll be here on Saturday. *(excitedly)* And on Sunday morning, we'll tie you to the rock and the dragon will come and bite through those ropes and fly you off to his cave. And you'll be trapped in the dark all alone until the Prince comes with his sword. Then comes the terrible fight and the Prince will be wounded, but he'll drive his sword home and the dragon will scream and thrash until it's dead. And the Prince will pull you from the dark cave and your dress will be torn from the dragon's claws and the Prince will be bloody from the dragon's teeth and you will return to the castle in triumph to be married. Oh! You're just growing up so fast! *(She pinches* **PRINCESS***'s cheek and exits.)*

PRINCESS. I'll be tied to a rock, then stuck in a dark cave, no sword, no dagger, completely helpless. I don't see why I have to wait for a prince to save me, when I'm certainly capable of slaying the dragon myself. I fence better than any man in the kingdom; it's just silly to not let me try. I'll speak to Daddy in the morning. He'll let me fight the dragon. He just has to!

Scene Three
The Garden

(**PRINCESS** *and* **KING** *enter the garden arm in arm.* **PRINCESS** *is carrying a basket of flowers. They sit.)*

KING. Such a lovely day. Seemed a shame to spend it cooped up in the castle signing proclamations. I'm glad you talked me into taking a walk.

PRINCESS. Thanks for walking with me. It is beautiful out here.

KING. And it gives me a chance to talk to you. After next week, I won't be seeing much of you anymore.

PRINCESS. I know. I wanted to talk about that, too.

KING. Just think, you'll be a queen in a brand new castle. The construction is almost done.

PRINCESS. Yes, I…

KING. Supervised it myself. Thirty-two bedrooms, alligators in the moat, two-car garage…

PRINCESS. Yes, I've seen it; it's lovely…

KING. And just wait 'til you see your husband.

PRINCESS. He's only my husband if he slays the dragon.

KING. Nonsense! Of course he'll slay the dragon. It's tradition.

PRINCESS. *(interrupts him)* But, Daddy, don't you think it's rather a silly tradition? You know I fence better than any of the boys in Middlefield. Couldn't we tie up the prince for the dragon to carry off – and then I could go and kill the dragon and rescue the Prince?

KING. The very idea! The Princess rescue the Prince? I realize you're handy with a sword, my dear, but surely…

PRINCESS. But think, Daddy. Wouldn't I be much safer with a sword in my hand? That way, if something terrible happens to the prince, I'll still be able to…

KING. Now listen my daughter. *(pulls puppets from his cloak)* The day your mother turned sixteen, her father tied her to a rock. At dawn, the dragon came – a fierce beast fifty feet in length with iron scales and teeth as sharp as knives. It swooped down, plucked your mother from the stone and flew off to its cave. *(fondly)* I can still hear your dear mother screaming in terror. Well, I followed the dreadful beast back to its lair and I fought. *(acts this out)* I parried; I thrusted; I advanced until it had nowhere to go. Then I raised my sword and…

PRINCESS. Where was Mother all this time?

KING. In the cave, of course, crying and wailing.

PRINCESS. But don't you see, Daddy, I don't want to just cry and wail and wait to be rescued. I want to do the rescuing myself.

KING. Since the beginning of time Princes have been rescuing Princesses from dragons, and Princes will continue to rescue Princesses from dragons until there are no dragons left in the world. And on Sunday, you will become part of that grand tradition. And I don't want to hear another word about it! *(exits)*

PRINCESS. I will fight that dragon. If I can't have a sword, I'll wrestle it with my bare hands. Tradition, indeed!

Scene Four
The Palace

*(***PRINCE*** and ***VALET*** enter, consulting a map.* **PRINCE** *is carrying a stack of books. He is thin and pale, with a studious manner.)*

VALET. Well, your highness, according to the map, this should be the right castle.

PRINCE. That's what you said three castles ago. Why should I believe you this time?

VALET. Well, sir, this time I'm not holding the map upside down.

PRINCE. Oh, give me that. *(He looks it over.)* Well, it looks as though this is the place. Oh, I can't go through with this! The Princess's beauty is known throughout the country. What if she doesn't like me? What if she takes one look at me and tells me to get right back in my motor car and go home? What if…?

VALET. Sir, maybe you should sit down.

(The **PRINCE** *sits. The* **VALET** *gives him a paper bag, which he breathes into.)*

Of course she'll like you. What's not to like? You've studied mathematics, philosophy, astronomy; you paint like Michelangelo and write poetry like Shakespeare. You're handsome, you drive a nice car, you have excellent table manners…

PRINCE. But I can't slay a dragon! And that's the only thing that matters. Oh, they should have picked Prince Brian the Burly.

VALET. Prince Brian has the brain of an apricot.

PRINCE. But the muscles of a…of a….

(He looks to the **VALET** *for help.* **VALET** *shrugs.)*

VALET. I got nothing.

PRINCE. Oh, I'm so nervous! I can't do this; I'm going home.

VALET. But I found all of these books for you. Surely there is something in there that will help.

PRINCE. I've read them all twice already. *101 Ways to Slay a Dragon, The Art of Slaying a Dragon, Dragonslaying For Dummies*...They won't do any good!

VALET. What's this one?

PRINCE. *(embarrassed) Men Who Slay Dragons and the Women Who Love Them.*

VALET. You can do this! You'll slay that dragon and you and the Princess will live happily ever after. I'm going to get the bags. *(exits)*

NURSE. *(enters)* Oh, excuse me, I didn't realize that anyone was in here, I...Wait! You wouldn't happen to be the... are you the...by any chance, would you be the...

PRINCE. The prince?

NURSE. You are the Prince! *(screams)* He's here! The Prince is here! *(to the* **PRINCE***)* Just wait till I tell the King! *(screams)* The Prince is here! *(to the* **PRINCE***)* The Prince is here! *(quieter)* Oh, but I guess you know that, seeing as you're the... *(runs offstage screaming)* The Prince is here!!!

VALET. *(enters with suitcases)* I heard screaming. Is everything all right?

PRINCE. I just met a charming lady. I believe she's going to fetch the others.

VALET. Splendid. Did she say how long that would take?

PRINCE. Not long, I imagine. Her voice seems to carry pretty far.

KING. *(enters)* Ah, the Prince! It's so good to meet you, son.

PRINCE. The pleasure is all mine, Your Highness.

KING. Oh, fiddlesticks! Call me Dad! Oh, you can't imagine how excited I am.

PRINCE. Oh, I think I can try.

KING. My daughter is on her way. I'll go hurry her along. *(exits)*

PRINCE. *(to* **VALET***)* I can't do this! I'm feeling a little sick.

VALET. You'll be fine.

PRINCE. I don't think I'm going to make it.

KING. *(enters)* Here she is. Sweetheart, come in here. May I present my daughter, the Princess of Middlefield.

PRINCESS. *(enters with* **NURSE***)* Your Highness, it's very nice to meet you; we have so much to talk about. Shall we... my goodness, are you all right?

PRINCE. I...I...oh dear! *(He runs offstage.)*

KING. Where is he going?

PRINCESS. Was it something I said?

VALET. A little motion sickness...nothing serious...I'll go check...make sure he's all right...*(He bumps into* **NURSE.***)* Well, hello there.

NURSE. Hello. Haven't seen you here before.

VALET. Just arrived. I'm with the Prince. Do you live here in the palace?

NURSE. Just up the stairs, third door from the...well, not that you can come up there...ladies section of the castle, you know...

VALET. Oh, yes...of course...wouldn't dream of it...and you are...?

NURSE. Nurse. And you are...

VALET. Valet.

NURSE. Oh.

*(***PRINCE** *is heard retching loudly offstage.)*

VALET. *(simultaneously)* I should go...

NURSE. *(simultaneously)* You should go...

VALET. I'll see you... *(He runs off stage.)*

PRINCESS. What was that?

KING. Motion sickness can be a terrible thing. I remember my first trip in a motor car; the chauffer was cleaning the backseat for weeks. I'll stop by the kitchen and have Cook send down a cup of tea. That'll do the trick. *(exits)*

PRINCESS. He's rather a pale-looking prince, don't you think?

NURSE. Prince? Oh, yes, the Prince. Can't say as I noticed. That Valet was strapping, though, wasn't he?

PRINCESS. Nurse, I need your help. I must speak to the Prince tonight.

NURSE. Tonight? Don't you think there'll be time enough for chatting once you're married?

PRINCESS. We'll never get married if he can't slay the dragon. He needs my help.

NURSE. Well, what are you standing around for? Let's go find the Prince!

Scene Five
The Palace

*(**PRINCE** and **VALET** enter.)*

PRINCE. I am so embarrassed!

VALET. Really, Your Highness, it wasn't so bad. They hardly noticed.

PRINCE. Hardly noticed? Hardly noticed?! It's all over – I'm going home. Get my bags.

VALET. Now don't be hasty. I'm sure of you just talk to the princess, everything will be fine.

PRINCE. *(directly into the **VALET**'s face)* Do you really think so?

VALET. *(overcome by the **PRINCE**'s horrible breath)* Absolutely. But not until we do something about your breath.

PRINCE. Oh no! Is it that bad?

PRINCESS. *(offstage)* Oh, prince? Are you in there? I must speak to you.

VALET. It's that bad. Run!

*(Pantomime – the **PRINCESS** and **NURSE** chase the **PRINCE** and **VALET** through the castle. Each time the **PRINCESS** comes upon them, the **PRINCE** hides and the **VALET** points them in a different direction. Each time, as the **PRINCESS** and **NURSE** leave, the **VALET** presents the **NURSE** with a gift – a flower, a small box of chocolates, a fruit basket. By the end of the chase, the **PRINCESS** is exhausted and the **NURSE** has her arms full of presents. The **PRINCESS** has not noticed the budding romance between the Nurse and Valet.)*

PRINCESS. That does it! I'll never talk to him at this rate.

NURSE. Don't give up hope, dear, we still haven't looked in the coat closet on the fourth floor.

PRINCESS. No, it's useless! By this time tomorrow, I'll have been eaten by a dragon. If you need me, I'll be in my chamber, writing my will.

NURSE. Chocolate?

PRINCESS. No thank you. *(double take)*

NURSE. *(mouth full)* Oooo! Why don't you write a letter instead?

PRINCESS. A suicide letter?

NURSE. No, luv, a letter to the Prince. Write him a letter, say you must meet with him tonight. I can give it to his Valet, explain the situation and you'll be speaking to the Prince by midnight.

PRINCESS. Midnight? It's only 6:00.

NURSE. Well, the Valet might need some convincing.

PRINCESS. All right. Back to my chamber! *(They exit.)*

Scene Six
The Palace

(The **PRINCE** *is sitting in his chamber, reading one of his self-help books, chewing on an enormous sprig of mint and parsley. The* **VALET** *rushes in out of breath with his hair mussed and lipstick kisses covering his face.)*

VALET. I have a note for you, sir. From the Princess.

PRINCE. The Princess? Where did you get this?

VALET. From her Nurse. The Princess has a plan, and I think you should meet her to discuss it.

PRINCE. *(reads the note)* She wants to meet at midnight? But it's nearly midnight now. Where have you been all this time?

VALET. Apparently, I needed some convincing.

PRINCE. Well, help me on with my coat.

VALET. *(helps him)* She'll be in the garden. Go! Go!

(The **PRINCE** *exits. The* **VALET** *watches him go, waits for a moment, then smoothes his hair and runs off to meet the* **NURSE**.*)*

Scene Seven
The Garden

(**PRINCESS** *is standing alone in the garden.* **PRINCE** *enters, holding the note and a rose.)*

PRINCE. There she is. Oh, she's so beautiful. What can I say? "Shall I compare thee to a summer's day?" No, that's silly. "How do I love thee? Let me count the ways." Oh, that won't work. I'll just be myself. I'll go right up to her and tell her how wonderful I think she is. I'll just walk over there and tap her on the shoulder and present her with this flower.

(He tiptoes over to her and lightly taps her shoulder. She mistakes him for an intruder and immediately flips him onto his back.)

PRINCESS. Hi-ya! *(realizes what she's done)* Oh no! I'm so sorry! Are you all right?

PRINCE. *(still on the ground)* Oh, yes. I'm fine.

PRINCESS. I thought you might be an intruder. Oh, I'm so sorry. Are you sure I didn't hurt you?

PRINCE. No really, I'm quite all right.

PRINCESS. Would you like some help getting up?

PRINCE. No, thank you. The stars are lovely this time of night; I think I'll just gaze at them a little longer.

PRINCESS. May I join you?

PRINCE. Of course. Make yourself comfortable.

(**PRINCESS** *lies down on the ground next to* **PRINCE**. *They look at the stars for a moment.* **PRINCE** *begins to laugh)*

PRINCESS. What are you laughing at?

PRINCE. Myself. I thought I'd be so romantic, taking you by surprise. I rather thought I'd sweep you off your feet.

(She laughs and helps him up to a seated position. He laughs with her.)

PRINCESS. My goodness, the stars are beautiful. Shall we sit here for a while?

PRINCE. By all means.

(They sit and look up at the stars. The **VALET** *and* **NURSE** *emerge from behind a bush, thinking the coast is clear. They see the* **PRINCE** *and* **PRINCESS** *and run offstage.)*

PRINCE. Andromeda is bright tonight.

PRINCESS. Where is it?

PRINCE. Right up there. No, a little to your left. That's it.

PRINCESS. It's beautiful.

PRINCE. Funny, Andromeda being so bright the night before we face our dragon.

PRINCESS. What do you mean?

PRINCE. Don't you know the story of Andromeda?

PRINCESS. The stars have stories?

PRINCE. Wonderful stories. With action and adventure and romance…

PRINCESS. Does Andromeda have action and adventure and romance?

PRINCE. With swords, and a battle and true love…

PRINCESS. Oh, please tell me!

PRINCE. I think you'll find it most entertaining. Long ago, King Cepheus and Queen Cassiopeia had a beautiful daughter named Andromeda. The Queen was a vain and boastful woman who claimed that she and her daughter were more beautiful even than the water nymphs, who were considered to be the loveliest creatures on earth. The nymphs heard about her boasts and grew very angry. They called on Poseidon, the God of the Seas, to punish her.

PRINCESS. My goodness! Did he?

PRINCE. Oh yes. Poseidon sent a horrible sea monster to destroy their kingdom.

PRINCESS. What did they do?

PRINCE. The King was told that the only way to save his kingdom was to sacrifice Andromeda to the sea monster. So he chained her to a rock near the sea and left her there.

PRINCESS. *(looks at him)* Are you making this up? You are, aren't you?

PRINCE. Not a bit. Why?

PRINCESS. It's just sounding a little familiar.

PRINCE. Do you want to hear the rest?

PRINCESS. Yes, please.

PRINCE. So Andromeda was chained to the rock, crying, and along came Perseus.

PRINCESS. Perseus?

PRINCE. The hero.

PRINCESS. Of course.

PRINCE. He took one look at the beautiful Andromeda and fell in love with her. She told him all about the monster and Perseus leaped into action.

PRINCESS. Did he slay the beast?

PRINCE. With one stroke of his sword. The King and Queen were so grateful to him for saving their daughter and their kingdom, they gave him Andromeda's hand in marriage.

PRINCESS. And they lived happily ever after?

PRINCE. That's what the story says.

PRINCESS. I guess my Nurse was right when she told me it was as old as the stars themselves. *(They smile.)* You tell it wonderfully. Do you know any other stories of the stars?

PRINCE. *(smiling)* I know the stories of all the constellations.

PRINCESS. Would you teach them to me sometime?

PRINCE. Of course. And would you...could you...I'm a little embarrassed to ask but...will you teach me how to wrestle?

PRINCESS. I would love to! You plant your feet and use your opponent's weight against him...

(She goes to throw the **PRINCE** *again.)*

PRINCE. Oh! I didn't mean right this minute. There will be plenty of time to learn when we're married.

PRINCESS. But, you know, we have to get past the dragon first.

PRINCE. Yes. The dragon. I've been reading up on this, and Prince Milo, the Mild-Mannered had a technique I'd like to try…

PRINCESS. You are the smartest prince I've ever met, but I'm afraid books won't help us against a dragon.

PRINCE. I was afraid of that.

PRINCESS. I have an idea. Tomorrow morning, after Father ties me to the rock, everyone will scurry home and put up the shutters until I've been rescued and the dragon has been slain.

PRINCE. What is your idea?

PRINCESS. Come out to the rock as soon as everyone has gone home. Bring my sword with you and cut me free. Then we can fight the dragon together. *(She holds out her hand.)*

PRINCE. *(takes her hand)* That is the most wonderful idea I have ever heard. I'll do it.

PRINCESS. I like you. After we slay the dragon, I'm looking forward to hearing more stories.

PRINCE. After we slay the dragon, we'll have a lifetime of stories.

Scene Eight
A Rock Outside the Palace

(The **KING** *enters with rope.)*

KING. My goodness, it's already first light. Where is she? The dragon won't wait forever.

(The **PRINCE** *enters, carrying two swords.)*

PRINCE. Oh! I didn't realize you would be...I mean...I thought the Princess...

KING. Not here yet. Fixing her hair, no doubt, or perhaps lifting weights.

PRINCE. She is a remarkable girl.

KING. Yes, she is. When her mother died, I'm afraid I didn't quite know how to raise a daughter. She's a bit...well, she's not a typical girl.

PRINCE. She's perfect.

KING. Yes, well...So are you all ready for the battle? Big day ahead of you and all.

PRINCE. Yes, I think so.

KING. I see you've brought two swords. Unusual technique but used with great success by Prince Ambrose the Ambidextrous.

PRINCE. Well I like to be prepared.

KING. Let me see one of those. *(He takes a sword.)* It's been a long time since I've held one of these.

(He takes a couple of swings, the **PRINCE** *ducks.)*

Feels good to have a strong bit of steel in my hand again. Ah, I remember when I went off to fight my dragon. Massive beast, one hundred feet from teeth to tail. I parried...

(He parries, the **PRINCE** *blocks his swing with great fear and just in time.)*

I thrusted...

(Again, the **PRINCE** *panicking by this time. The* **KING** *begins to fight as he describes the action, backing the*

PRINCE *in a circle and across the stage. The* **PRINCE** *is desperately blocking each blow.)*

KING. *(cont.)* Such a fight it was! We circled the cave, the dragon blocking me at every turn. I stabbed his throat, I slashed his chest, but to no avail. It was the largest dragon ever recorded, and the strongest, too. Then, just when it was looking bleak for me, I gave a mighty swing, the dragon roared…

(In a full panic by this time, the **PRINCE** *yells in fear at the top of his lungs and begins to wildly slash his sword, accidentally, and luckily, disarming the* **KING**. *He begins to hyperventilate.)*

Well done, my boy, well done! The shouting is a nice touch…puts some fear into the enemy.

PRINCE. Yes, well, there's nothing like a little fear…*(continues to pant heavily)*

NURSE. *(offstage)* Move along, luv, the rock is just around this bend.

KING. Ah, it's my daughter! You'd better move along son, it's bad luck to see the bride before the slaughter. *(hands him the extra sword)*

PRINCE. Of course. I'll be right over there behind those trees. Waiting for the screaming. *(exits)*

*(***NURSE** *and* **PRINCESS** *enter.* **NURSE** *is looking very tired.)*

KING. Daughter, dear, please hurry it along. We mustn't keep the dragon waiting.

NURSE. Yes, please, let's do this quickly. I barely slept at all last night. *(***PRINCESS** *looks at her.)* All the excitement. Gives me heartburn.

PRINCESS. All right. If it's my duty to be dragon food, I might as well get it over with. Do you think he'll swallow me whole, or will I be marinated with herbs and a dry sherry?

KING. Oh, don't be so dramatic. I've never seen a prince fail. Of course, I've never seen a prince vomit, either, but have no fear. This prince is a good egg. Very bright, I hear. Speaks six languages…

PRINCESS. Seven.

KING. Knows all about astrology…

PRINCESS. Astronomy.

NURSE. Not to mention his excellent taste in servants.

(They look at her – she smooths her skirt.)

KING. Everything will be fine. You'll see. Why, I remember when I slew my dragon. *(pulls out puppets again, gives one to the* **NURSE***)* It seems like only yesterday. A monster, he was, one hundred feet in length, with iron scales and razor sharp claws. He came toward me with his teeth bared, ready to strike. I took out my sword; I parried…I thrusted…

*(***PRINCE** *enters.* **PRINCESS** *shoos him away. He exits.)*

PRINCESS. I'm sure you're right, Daddy. *(loudly, so the* **PRINCE** *can hear)* And thank you, for selecting such a kind, intelligent, understanding Prince. I like him very much and I'm certain he will conduct himself most gallantly today.

KING. Oh, well, I have only your best interests at heart, my sweet. Now, let's get you tied up!

(They begin to tie her to the rope.)

NURSE. Is this too tight, luv?

PRINCESS. No, it's just fine, thank you.

NURSE. We wouldn't want to strangle you before the dragon gets a crack at it!

PRINCESS. I appreciate that.

KING. Well, it seems plenty secure. *(tugs at the rope)* I guess we'll head back to the castle.

NURSE. You take care of yourself, luv.

KING. Don't forget to wail and cry. Tradition, you know.

PRINCESS. I'll try to remember. Don't worry. I'll be home before you even notice I'm gone.

*(***KING** *and* **NURSE** *exit, calling goodbyes.* **PRINCE** *begins to enter,* **NURSE** *runs back in with sweater,* **PRINCE** *runs off.)*

NURSE. In case it gets cold in the cave.

(She tries to put the sweater on **PRINCESS,** *but can't get it around the ropes. She leaves it apologetically on the rock and exits.)*

PRINCE. Is everyone gone?

PRINCESS. Yes. Untie me quickly – the dragon will be here any minute.

PRINCE. *(untying her)* I brought your sword. Here.

PRINCESS. Thank you. *(She takes the sword.)* Now all we have to do is wait for the dragon.

PRINCE. Right. Does he come along fairly quickly?

PRINCESS. Oh, yes. Get your sword ready.

(They wait with their swords poised. Nothing happens.)

PRINCE. You're sure he knows that this is the day.

PRINCESS. Of course. Dragons have a sixth sense about these things. They always know when it's the sixteenth birthday of a princess.

PRINCE. Is that it? *(They raise their swords.)*

PRINCESS. No, just a bird.

(They wait. **PRINCE** *sees something and starts swinging his sword wildly, ending by banging it repeatedly against the rock.* **PRINCESS** *stares at him.)*

PRINCE. Dragonfly.

PRINCESS. Ah. Did you...?

PRINCE. It's dead.

PRINCESS. Well done.

(They sit on the rock and wait some more.)

PRINCE. I don't think the dragon is coming.

PRINCESS. I think you might be right. He could have gotten his days mixed up.

PRINCE. I can't imagine he keeps a calendar.

PRINCESS. I suppose we'll have to go and find him.

PRINCE. Do you know where to look?

PRINCESS. I haven't the faintest idea.

(They look around on the ground and in the air. The **PRINCE** *notices something.)*

PRINCE. Look at this! Tracks! Look, that's where he's dragged his brass tail and planted his steel claws.

PRINCESS. Let's go get him!

(She starts offstage. He pulls out paper bag and begins breathing into it. She returns)

What are you waiting for?

PRINCE. Just give me a minute. I'm all right now. We are together, and that makes everything all right. Let's get in my motor car and follow the tracks up the hill.

(He takes her hand and they exit.)

Scene Nine
Outside the Dragon's Cave

*(**PRINCE** and **PRINCESS** enter.)*

PRINCE. Do you think he's in there?

PRINCESS. I don't know. Should we call him?

PRINCE. I suppose. Should we draw our swords?

PRINCESS. Absolutely. *(They draw their swords)* I'm going to call him. Dragon!

PRINCE. What ho! Dragon!

*(There is a creaking and rattling sound from inside the cave. The **PRINCE** and **PRINCESS** look at each other and take hands.)*

PRINCESS. Dragon! I say – Dragon! Do come out and talk to us. We've brought you a present!

DRAGON. *(from offstage)* Oh yes – I know your presents! One of those precious princesses, I suppose? And I've got to come out and fight for her. Well, I'll tell you straight, I'm not going to do it.

PRINCE. Not going to do it?

PRINCESS. But why? It's...it's...well, it's tradition.

DRAGON. *(from offstage)* Tradition! I'll tell you about this tradition! For centuries I've watched dragons get killed by princes. I've stayed out of it all these years, and I'm staying out of it now.

PRINCE. *(to **PRINCESS**)* Well, as much as I don't want to, we have to fight a dragon or they won't let us get married. And I really would like to marry you.

PRINCESS. I'd like that, too. Do you suppose he knows of another dragon in the area?

PRINCE. We can ask. Dragon! Would you know where we could find, maybe, another dragon?

DRAGON. There aren't any.

PRINCESS. It doesn't have to be close by. We have a motor car – we can travel a good distance.

DRAGON. You could travel to the ends of the earth – you still won't find another dragon. I'm the only one left.

PRINCE. The only one?

PRINCESS. In the world?

DRAGON. *(from offstage)* Yes! I'm the only living dragon left in the world, and I'd like to stay living. So go away and leave me alone! *(There is rattling and creaking.)*

PRINCE. Imagine! The last of the dragons.

PRINCESS. I had no idea.

PRINCE. Well, we can't kill it. It's the last one.

PRINCESS. But we can't just go home without a dragon.

PRINCE. That's it! We'll go home with a dragon! We'll tame it!

PRINCESS. What a wonderful idea! How do you tame a dragon?

PRINCE. I have no idea. I don't believe anyone's ever written a book on the subject.

PRINCESS. They say animals can be tamed by kindness, but perhaps that's just domestic animals, like dogs and crocodiles. I don't know if it would work with dragons.

PRINCE. I suppose anything is worth a try. Taming by kindness means giving him things to eat. Have you got anything to eat?

PRINCESS. Not a thing. Have you?

PRINCE. Oh! I have some biscuits in the car. Breakfast was so early, and I thought we might be feeling a little faint after the fight. I'll go get them. *(He exits.)*

PRINCESS. He is indeed the most clever Prince I've ever met. I'm so glad Daddy picked him and not Prince Brian. Of course, Prince Brian is strong, but he has the brains of an apricot.

PRINCE. *(enters)* Here they are.

PRINCESS. Dragon! Do you like biscuits?

DRAGON. *(offstage)* No!

PRINCESS. Not even the nice little expensive ones with sugar on top?

DRAGON. *(offstage)* No!

PRINCESS. Then what do you like?

DRAGON. *(offstage)* Nothing! Now go away!

PRINCESS. He must like something. Dragon! Dragon dear!

DRAGON. *(offstage)* WHAT? Say that again! *(clattering and banging)*

PRINCESS. *(The* **PRINCE** *grabs her hand.)* Dragon – Dragon dear!

(The rattling becomes louder. The **PRINCESS** *starts to raise her sword, but the* **PRINCE** *stops her. They back up slowly. The dragon emerges from the cave spreading her wings. She is crying.)*

PRINCESS. My goodness, he's crying.

PRINCE. And "he's" a "she."

DRAGON. Of course I'm a she…you didn't think there were only boy dragons did you?

PRINCE. Well…of course not. I guess I just thought that with dragons being such strong fighters and all they must be… *(looks at* **PRINCESS***)* Uh…never mind.

PRINCESS. But Dragon, whatever is the matter?

DRAGON. Nobody ever called me "dear" before!

PRINCESS. Don't cry. We'll call you "dear" as often as you like. We want to tame you.

DRAGON. I am tame – that's just it. That's what nobody has ever bothered to find out. All of us dragons were tame.

PRINCE. All of you?

DRAGON. Of course. We mostly kept to ourselves in our caves. Sometimes we'd go out to stretch our wings, but we were always careful to fly at night so as not to frighten anyone. Then one morning long ago, outside London, a young dragon was flying home and he saw a young princess tied to a rock. There was a sign next to her that read, "For the dragon." Well, he thought, that was very kind of the little girl to offer to keep him company, so he bit gently through the ropes and carried her back to his cave.

PRINCESS. He wasn't going to eat her?

DRAGON. Heaven's no! He was only going to offer her a cup of tea, toast a few marshmallows, maybe tell a story by the fire. But he had barely arrived home when a muscle-bound, sword-wielding hulk of a prince burst into his cave and killed him on the spot!

PRINCESS. How terrible!

PRINCE. But if you all knew you'd be slain for kidnapping, why did you continue to take the princesses from the rock?

DRAGON. Dragons are a trusting lot. And we're very lonely. We could never understand why you humans would give us princesses to play with, then barge in and snatch them right back. It hardly seemed fair.

PRINCESS. It isn't fair. It's terrible. On behalf of royalty everywhere, I'm so sorry.

PRINCE. So you never wanted to eat us?

DRAGON. I would never eat a human. Yuck! So stringy, too many bones, and the taste...Ugh!

PRINCESS. I'm glad you won't eat us. But are you sure you won't have a biscuit?

DRAGON. No. I don't care for biscuits.

PRINCESS. What then, dragon dear?

DRAGON. Your kindness quite undragons me. No one has ever asked any of us what we like to eat – always offering us princesses and then rescuing them – and never once "What'll you take to drink the King's health?" Cruel hard, I call it.

PRINCE. Well, today is a celebration. We're to be married today, aren't we Princess?

PRINCESS. Yes, we are. What will you take to drink our health?

DRAGON. What'll I take to drink your health? I'd be proud to drink your and your good lady's health in a little drop of – to think of you asking me so friendly like – yes, sir, just a little drop of p...p...p...p...petrol. That's what does a dragon good, sir.

PRINCE. Petrol! Why I have barrels of it in the car!

PRINCESS. Barrels? Why so much for such a short trip?

PRINCE. Oh, well, you know...in case I lost my nerve... I would have needed to go far away...but I packed them before I met you, of course. I'll go get them out of the car. *(exits)*

DRAGON. If I might make so bold, while the gentleman's away – if you could be so kind as to shake claws with me – well, the last of the dragons'll be the proudest dragon there's ever been since the first of them.

(He holds out his claw. The **PRINCESS** *takes it.)*

PRINCESS. Dragon, dear, may I ask you a question?

DRAGON. Of course, Princess. You may ask me anything you like.

PRINCESS. Oh, dragon, will you come to the castle and live with us forever? It's a beautiful castle, warm and dry, with alligators in the moat and a two-car garage. You could be our protector and companion, and we will always call you dear.

DRAGON. I would be honored to be your friend, and I will protect you and your children and your children's children for the rest of my days.

Scene Ten
The Palace

KING. They should have been back by now.

NURSE. Now I'm sure everything is just fine.

VALET. You don't know the Prince very well.

NURSE. Now don't lose hope. The Prince and Princess will be here any minute and we can start celebrating.

KING. I'm sure you're right. Ah, the air is thick with excitement! I haven't felt this alive since the day I set out to rescue the Queen. *(brings out puppets)* What a fight that was! A dragon two hundred feet in length – it was the largest, meanest dragon we had ever seen – with iron scales and fiery breath! He scorched through my armor, but I stood my ground. I drew my trusty sword; I parried...I thrusted...

(There is a rumbling and clattering heard offstage.)

KING. What in the world is that?

NURSE. It sounds as if the whole castle is falling down!

VALET. I'll protect you! *(He jumps on top of her.)*

(The noise gets louder and louder until the **DRAGON** *enters. Everyone screams and jumps to their feet.)*

KING. The dragon!

NURSE. The dragon!

VALET. The dragon!

KING. The beast has eaten my daughter!

NURSE. We'll all be killed!

VALET. Protect me! *(He jumps into her arms.)*

(The **PRINCE** *and* **PRINCESS** *run in.)*

PRINCE. Don't be afraid!

PRINCESS. She's not going to hurt you!

KING. But it's a dragon. Dragons eat royalty! Where is my sword? My kingdom for a sword! I'll parry! I'll...thrust!

PRINCESS. No, Daddy, wait! She's a tame dragon.

VALET. A tame dragon?

PRINCESS. Yes.

KING. A "She?"

NURSE. There's no such thing as a tame dragon.

PRINCE. Listen to us! She is the very last dragon in the world. We couldn't hurt her.

PRINCESS. She is kind and sweet. All the dragons were kind and sweet. All they ever wanted was a princess to be a friend and to tell stories by the fire. I have decided to be her friend. And I've named her Fido.

DRAGON. I know it's a bit of a shock, having a dragon drop in like this, but Your Highness, I wouldn't ever hurt your daughter. I'd like to stay and join in the wedding celebration.

PRINCESS. May she stay, Father?

KING. *(silence for a moment)* The very last dragon?

PRINCESS. The very last one.

KING. May I have a word with the dragon? In private?

PRINCESS. Of course. *(They move away.)*

KING. Tame dragon, eh?

DRAGON. All of us.

KING. So how well did you know the other dragons?

DRAGON. I saw them around every now and then.

KING. There was one, about thirty years ago…lived in a cave by the sea…two days journey by horse.

DRAGON. Yes, I remember. Tragic story that was. On his way back from picking up the princess, he flew right into a mountain. Died on the spot. From what I heard, that princess was very lucky. Got through without a scratch. We all figured it was because that dragon was such a tiny one. Didn't make too much of a crash when he fell.

KING. Yes, well, about that…would it be too much trouble to keep that story to yourself? It would mean a great deal to me.

DRAGON. Of course, your Highness. I will never repeat it again.

KING. Thank you. *(to others)* Of course she can stay! My dear Fido, let me pour you a cup of wine!

PRINCE. Actually, she'll take a barrel of petrol.

KING. Well, what are you all just standing there for? Get this dragon a barrel of petrol! *(all cheer)* Now, I believe we have a wedding to attend.

PRINCESS. Father, I have chosen a maid of honor.

KING. Finally. I'll send a messenger down to the village. Which girl is it?

PRINCESS. You don't need to send the messenger. She isn't from the village. I've chosen my very best friend and companion. Nurse? Will you be my maid of honor?

NURSE. Oh! Princess! I'd be delighted!

PRINCE. *(to* **VALET***)* And you will be my best man.

VALET. Nothing could make me happier. Except for one thing.

PRINCE. What's that?

VALET. If this lovely lady would be my bride. *(gets on one knee in front of the* **NURSE***)* Will you marry me?

NURSE. Oh! Yes!

DRAGON. *(raises her barrel of petrol)* To the happy couples!

ALL. To the happy couples!

PRINCESS. Oh, Fido! What a wonderful dragon you are!

(They freeze in tableau.)

STORYTELLER. When the Prince and Princess were settled in their own kingdom, Fido came to them and begged to be allowed to make herself useful. So the Prince had a special saddle made for her with one hundred and fifty seats attached to it. And the dragon, whose greatest pleasure was now to give pleasure to others, delighted in taking parties of children to the seaside. The children were very fond of her and called her "dear" – a word that never failed to bring tears to her eyes. So there she lived out her days – useful, respected, and very, very loved.

The End.

Also by

Kristin Walter...

The Elves and the Shoemaker

Hansel & Gretel

Rapunzel

The Selfish Giant

TITLES AVAILABLE FROM SAMUEL FRENCH

HANSEL & GRETEL

Book and Lyrics by Kristin Walter
Music by Michael Walter and Karen Biscopink

Musical/3f, 1m/multiple settings

In this twist on the classic fairy tale, Hansel and Gretel are actually "Hank and Gertie," two poor children from the hills of Appalachia. When a witch moves in to town and puts their parents under a spell, these intrepid siblings must outsmart and defeat her. A musical, this version of the story is set to a beautiful bluegrass score.

"*Hansel and Gretel* may not be the one the Brothers Grimm envisioned, but it works better as children's theatre."
- *Off-Off Broadway Review*

"(The) bluegrass score, filled with energetic fiddling and earnest ballads, also leavens the proceedings. But it never seems out of place. What could be better than country music for a tale of backwoods hope and betrayal."
- *New York Times* S

TITLES AVAILABLE FROM SAMUEL FRENCH

THE SELFISH GIANT

Book by Kristin Walter
Music and Lyrics by Larisa Bryski

Musical / 5f, 4m or 3f, 2m with doubling / Unit Set

When four bored children decide to play in the Giant's garden, they are in for a nasty surprise. The Giant builds a fence to keep them out, and threatens anyone who tries to come in. But when winter comes and sees that no one is having any fun, it decides to stay forever. It's up to the new girl in town to take down the fence and teach the Giant a lesson in friendship. Based on the story by Oscar Wilde.

"*The Selfish Giant* is a kids' show, but the theme is universal. Its simple message may influence your child, but its affect on you may be refreshingly unexpected."
- *The Tribeca Tribune*

"Kristin Walter's charming adaptation of Oscar Wilde's fairy tale about a giant who builds a wall around his arden so no children can play there is as relevant for millennial children as it was to Wilde's Victorian readers."
- *Off-Off Broadway Review*

"Larisa Bryski's songs will delight theatergoers 3 to 9 years old."
- *The New York Times*

TITLES AVAILABLE FROM SAMUEL FRENCH

RAPUNZEL

Kristin Walter and Michael Walter

Musical / 2m, 3f / multiple settings

In this twist on the classic fairy tale, Rapunzel is snatched from her parents on the night of her birth by the evil witch who lives next door and is raised in a tower for sixteen years. The beautiful young woman finds her prince, but he turns out to be quite different than she expected; he is her twin brother! Together, they defeat the witch and are reunited with their true parents.

"In addition to the comedy, children will enjoy Michael Walter's pop score"
- *The New York Times*

"Michael Walter's tuneful music relays the message of endurance and love conveyed by (Kristin) Walter's lyrics." - *Off-Off Broadway Review*

TITLES AVAILABLE FROM SAMUEL FRENCH

THE ELVES AND THE SHOEMAKER

Kristin Walter

Comedy / 3f, 2m / multiple settings

Unfortunately, Eric, the lone shoemaker of Grimmsville, makes shoes that are miserably uncomfortable and impossible to walk in...leaving a lot of barefoot villagers and Eric without a means to provide for his family. While his wife tries to be supportive, his daughter Shannon just can't take it anymore! Sitting alone in the woods pondering her family's fate, Shannon is confronted by a stranger who offers her the deal of a lifetime... in exchange for her torturous pair of shoes, she is given a magical medallion that holds "the charm of the elves." Wanting to help her family, Shannon tries the chant. Her words beckon a pair of elves that show up night after night at the shoemaker's home creating the most fabulous shoes EVER! With his shoes now wanted throughout the land, Eric and his family have more gold than they can count. But they quickly begin to realize that all the money in the world doesn't necessarily buy happiness.

"...the script by Kristin Walter is a joy - true to the original story, but with enough clever asides to keep the parents in the audience laughing along with the kids."
- *nytheatre.com*

"Walter is a clever playwright. She masterfully writes one line for the children to enjoy and follows it up with a quick-witted one that seems to nudge the parent in the rib."
- *Off-Off Broadway Review*

TITLES AVAILABLE FROM SAMUEL FRENCH

JACK AND THE SOY BEANSTALK

Book and Lyrics by Jerrod Bogard
Music by Sky Seals and Emily Fellner

TYA, Children's Musical / 6m, 2f, possible doubling

Follow Jack up the beanstalk once more in this zany, 45-minute musical romp! Times have changed though, and Jack faces new obstacles on his journey - like how to make his truck go without gasoline and how to stop his mother from selling off his precious video games! Jack learns sometimes you have to take a leap of faith, but that when you do, you have to be prepared for anything - like maybe, oh…a giant! But in this modern-day fable the giant isn't just some tall guy in the clouds. He's the C.E.O. of a "giant" farming corporation: Big Aggie Reaping Farms (B.A.R.F.).

Through his battle with the Giant, Jack discovers that greed consumes itself, and that only through the help of our neighbors will we all prosper. Filled with comedy, puppetry, and lots of heart, *Jack and the Soy Beanstalk* plants the seeds of self-reliance, conservationism, and good ol' American ingenuity.

" Does not disappoint on any level..fast-paced and energetic!"
- *NYTheatre.com*

" A rip-roaring good time musical with a light-hearted green message. This is a must see masterpiece for all ages."
- *TheaterOnline.com*

" Wonderfully entertaining for both the kids and the adults."
- *StageBuzz.com*

SAMUEL FRENCH STAFF

Nate Collins
President

Ken Dingledine
Director of Operations,
Vice President

Bruce Lazarus
Executive Director,
General Counsel

Rita Maté
Director of Finance

ACCOUNTING

Lori Thimsen | Director of Licensing Compliance
Nehal Kumar | Senior Accounting Associate
Glenn Halcomb | Royalty Administration
Jessica Zheng | Accounts Receivable
Andy Lian | Accounts Payable
Charlie Sou | Accounting Associate
Joann Mannello | Orders Administrator

BUSINESS AFFAIRS

Caitlin Bartow | Assistant to the Executive Director

CORPORATE COMMUNICATIONS

Abbie Van Nostrand | Director of Corporate Communications

CUSTOMER SERVICE AND LICENSING

Brad Lohrenz | Director of Licensing Development
Laura Lindson | Licensing Services Manager
Kim Rogers | Theatrical Specialist
Matthew Akers | Theatrical Specialist
Ashley Byrne | Theatrical Specialist
Jennifer Carter | Theatrical Specialist
Annette Storckman | Theatrical Specialist
Dyan Flores | Theatrical Specialist
Sarah Weber | Theatrical Specialist
Nicholas Dawson | Theatrical Specialist
David Kimple | Theatrical Specialist

EDITORIAL

Amy Rose Marsh | Literary Manager
Ben Coleman | Literary Associate

MARKETING

Ryan Pointer | Marketing Manager
Courtney Kochuba | Marketing Associate
Chris Kam | Marketing Associate

PUBLICATIONS AND PRODUCT DEVELOPMENT

Joe Ferreira | Product Development Manager
David Geer | Publications Manager
Charlyn Brea | Publications Associate
Tyler Mullen | Publications Associate
Derek P. Hassler | Musical Products Coordinator
Zachary Orts | Musical Materials Coordinator

OPERATIONS

Casey McLain | Operations Supervisor
Elizabeth Minski | Office Coordinator, Reception
Coryn Carson | Office Coordinator, Reception

SAMUEL FRENCH BOOKSHOP (LOS ANGELES)

Joyce Mehess | Bookstore Manager
Cory DeLair | Bookstore Buyer
Sonya Wallace | Bookstore Associate
Tim Coultas | Bookstore Associate
Alfred Contreras | Shipping & Receiving

LONDON OFFICE

Anne-Marie Ashman | Accounts Assistant
Felicity Barks | Rights & Contracts Associate
Steve Blacker | Bookshop Associate
David Bray | Customer Services Associate
Robert Cooke | Assistant Buyer
Stephanie Dawson | Amateur Licensing Associate
Simon Ellison | Retail Sales Manager
Robert Hamilton | Amateur Licensing Associate
Peter Langdon | Marketing Manager
Louise Mappley | Amateur Licensing Associate
James Nicolau | Despatch Associate
Martin Phillips | Librarian
Panos Panayi | Company Accountant
Zubayed Rahman | Despatch Associate
Steve Sanderson | Royalty Administration Supervisor
Douglas Schatz | Acting Executive Director
Roger Sheppard | I.T. Manager
Debbie Simmons | Licensing Sales Team Leader
Peter Smith | Amateur Licensing Associate
Garry Spratley | Customer Service Manager
David Webster | UK Operations Director
Sarah Wolf | Rights Director

SAMUELFRENCH.COM
SAMUELFRENCH-LONDON.CO.UK